CREEPERS

⭐ ⭐ ⭐ ⭐ ⭐

—Sydney V., 9, Murfreesboro

"These books are good stories that you will want to read.
Not too creepy, but scary enough!"

—Owen H., 10, Mansfield

"Creepers is an amazing series that keeps me turning pages
well past my bedtime (sorry mom)!"

—@pageturningpatrick, 11, Collingwood

"I wanted to keep reading, I didn't know what was going to happen
next! It was exciting and creepy all at the same time!"

—Avery H., 12, Hamilton

"Creepers is creepy, fun, and a bit mesmerizing!"

—Clara H., 10, Burlington

"The suspense kept me going! I can't wait to read the next book!!"

—Francesca N., 12, Jackson Heights

"The characters are very intriguing, and the ending
of the book was unpredictable."

—Abby, 11, Murfreesboro

"Those of the younger audience will get a cold shiver
down their back while reading this book,
as the same happened to me once or twice."

—Cameron, 13, Smyrna

"The content and ideas are
DARK, THRILLING, SPINE-CHILLING, GRUESOME
at times, extremely interesting, and sometimes even hilarious."

—Marla Conn, M.S. Ed., reading and literacy specialist
and educational consultant

Ghost Writer

by Edgar J. Hyde

Illustrations by Chloe Tyler

PAB-0608-0309 • ISBN: 978-1-4867-2126-9

Made in China/Fabriqué en Chine

NOV 2 4 2021

Table of Contents

CHAPTER ONE

The New House

It was late Saturday afternoon and verging on evening. Charlie, Kate, and Neil were all packing for the move. They had been busy clearing up the last few things in their rooms before the final moving van took the last of their possessions to the new house.

Charlie was the oldest at fifteen. His hair was parted down the center and he had a very rugged look about him. Kate was of average height with medium-long hair and dark, mysterious eyes. She was fourteen. Neil was thirteen and was about the same height as his sister. He had dark brown eyes and short, thick hair.

The teens were moving to a bigger, older house with a huge backyard on the other side of town.

"Oh no! No!" cried Neil from his bedroom. Charlie and Kate rushed into his room.

"What's up?" asked Charlie.

"I can't find my video games!" answered Neil.

"You packed them already, remember?" said Kate. "You put them in a box outside your door."

"Oh yeah," remembered Neil in relief.

"You bonehead!" said Charlie. "Don't scare me like that."

"Come on, kids!" called Dad from downstairs. "Get your stuff together. We're leaving!"

"Coming!" called Neil.

"Yeah, coming!" called Charlie and Kate.

Charlie took one more look at his now empty bedroom before picking up the last box full of his possessions and walking downstairs.

"Come on, Charlie," called Neil who was already in the car with Kate, "we're going!"

"Coming," replied Charlie, quickly lobbing his box haphazardly into the back of the moving van. He then leapt into the back of the car as Dad started the engine and drove off.

They arrived at the new house at half past eight and, as it was late fall, it was pitch black. The house was on the other side of town and was much bigger than the one they had just left. It was also older. The walls were in serious need of repair. The windows were tall with pointed arches and reflected the glare of the car's headlights as it turned into the drive. Dad had been doing the more important repair jobs the past two months, but the house was still in need of considerable renovation.

The teenagers clambered out of the car and followed their parents up the path to the front door. Dad fumbled with the key in the lock.

"I haven't gotten around to oiling it yet," he said with a laugh.

They all walked onto the porch and Charlie shut the door behind him. He had to push it closed with some force.

Dad fumbled for the light switch. Upon finding it, he flicked it up. The lights came on for a few seconds until they flickered and then died out.

"Darn!" exclaimed Dad. "I'll work on the fuse box. Charlie, go get the flashlight from the car."

"Okay, Dad," replied Charlie.

Charlie took the keys from his dad and opened the front door again. He walked down the path until he reached the car. He put the key in the lock and turned it. Upon hearing the sound of the motors of the central lock whirring, he opened the rear-left door and took the flashlight from the pocket behind the front seat.

He tested it quickly, then he locked the car and hurried back inside.

When he had closed the front door behind him, he found only his dad waiting there.

"Where are the others?" asked Charlie as he handed the keys back to his father.

"They're in the kitchen," replied Dad. "You might as well join them and help make some food—I can figure out this fuse box by myself. You go on and see if they need help."

"Okay," answered Charlie as he handed his dad the flashlight.

In the kitchen he found the gas burner on, giving the room a bit of light and Neil trying to get a fire going in the ancient fireplace. Kate and Mom were sitting across from each other talking quietly at the old kitchen table which had come with the house. Charlie sat down next to Mom and idly watched Neil trying to get the fire started.

"You're not going to be able to do it," he taunted.

"How much do you wanna bet?" replied Neil.

"I think five bucks will do nicely—I bet that you won't get the fire going before the electricity's back on," replied Charlie.

"You're on," answered Neil.

Over the next ten minutes, Charlie watched as Neil tried to get the fire started.

Suddenly, with no warning, a light flickered in the hallway from the direction of the porch. The light dimmed, then steadied itself out and remained constant.

"Five dollars, please," said Charlie smugly.

"Fine. That's the last time I ever make a bet with you," replied Neil, handing the five-dollar bill over to Charlie.

"We're even now—remember yesterday when I lost that bet to you?" said Charlie.

"You guys shouldn't keep betting," said Kate. "You're just going to lose all your money."

"Or win it," said Charlie with a grin.

Neil laughed. "Maybe she's got a point though, Charlie. I do always lose."

"Then don't bet," answered Charlie as Dad walked into the kitchen.

"All right then, family. Do you want food or do you just want to go to bed?" he asked.

"Food!" replied the teenagers.

After a quick meal they went to their chosen rooms and fell into their beds. Thankfully the movers had already brought those over the day before. They were all asleep almost as soon as their heads touched their pillows.

The next morning, Charlie was the first one to wake up. He showered and got dressed. It was half past eight and there was nothing to do, so he decided to start work on his latest short story for the school magazine. He loved the magazine. He wrote a new story for each issue. The stories took up only a page in the magazine, but Charlie hoped to write a whole novel one day. At the moment, he was doing a series so he was writing a story for several issues ahead.

He sat down with his pen and notebook and

thought for a while. Then he began writing.

At half past nine, Neil peered into his room and said, "Morning, Charlie. It's time for breakfast."

"I'll be down in a second," replied Charlie.

Charlie finished writing the sentence he was working on. He placed his pen neatly next to the notebook and stood up.

Down in the kitchen, Dad was serving up eggs, bacon, sausages, and hash browns onto the plates laid out around the old, worn kitchen table.

He looked up as Neil entered, followed shortly by Charlie.

"Good morning, Charlie!" greeted Dad cheerfully. "Sleep well?"

"Yeah," replied Charlie, "and you?"

"Fine, thanks," answered Dad, sitting down at his place next to Mom. "Where's Kate?"

"She'll be down any minute," said Neil while also sitting down. "What are we doing today?"

"Well, as it's the first day of your week-long

vacation, I thought you might like to give us a hand unpacking," said Dad.

"Great," said Kate unenthusiastically as she entered the kitchen.

"You sound excited, Kate," said Charlie.

"Great," repeated Kate a little more enthusiastically as she saw the contents of the kitchen table, "a tasty breakfast—just what I need."

"I thought that might cheer you up," said Dad, smiling, "and I'm glad you eventually decided to join us."

Kate grinned and sat down at the empty space left for her at the table.

For a few minutes nobody talked as they scarfed down their breakfast. Eventually Dad sat back, wiped his face with a napkin, and let out a happy sigh. "I really needed that," he said with a contented smile.

The teenagers cleared the table and washed up while Mom and Dad got dressed for the day.

By eleven o'clock, everyone was ready to start unpacking everything from their old house.

The furniture had been unpacked a few days earlier. All the family had to do was unpack their personal possessions.

The teenagers began to unpack their own boxes and put things away. By six o'clock, they had almost finished personalizing their bedrooms. They decided to call it a day and finish up tomorrow.

After dinner, Charlie tried to finish his short story.

By nine thirty he decided to go to bed early. Charlie set his pen and notebook next to his bed and read the last few words to himself.

James knelt down and tried to pry the lid off of the box, but it was stuck.

As he lay in bed, he wondered how he could continue the plot. He was still mulling it over as he fell sound asleep.

CHAPTER TWO

Haunted House

"Wake up, Charlie!"

Charlie sat up and rubbed his eyes. "What?" he asked, still half asleep.

"I said, wake up, Charlie!" said Neil, standing in the doorway. "It's nine o'clock."

"Okay, okay," replied Charlie, shaking his head and wondering why he hadn't woken up earlier. It wasn't like him to sleep for twelve hours.

He glanced at his bedside clock to see if it really was nine o'clock. As his gaze swept across his bedside table, he happened to notice his notebook. Without really knowing why, he picked the notebook up and read the last few words.

Suddenly, the lid flew open and James's hand slipped. His hand caught on one of the nails sticking from the side of the box. He clutched his hand as blood began to seep through a gash in his index finger.

Charlie sat there for a few seconds, taken aback by the words that he could not remember adding to the end of his story the night before. He shrugged thinking that he must have woken up and written it in the middle of the night. Maybe that was why he woke up so late this morning?

Charlie put the notebook back on the table and got out of bed. What he hadn't noticed was that although he had written the story with a ballpoint pen yesterday, the new sentence, while in his own handwriting, was written in fountain pen ink.

Breakfast was not as elaborate as the day before. Charlie had cornflakes with a glass of orange juice. After breakfast, he unpacked and sorted the rest of his things before helping his parents place all of the kitchen items into their correct drawers and cabinets.

By half past four, Charlie and his parents had finished organizing the kitchen and were ready to tackle cleaning the rest of the house. Kate and Neil helped out with this and by eight o'clock they were halfway through the job. After a very constructive day working together, the family decided to finish work for the day and Mom and Dad began to make dinner. Charlie, Kate, and Neil played cards in the large dining room. The dining room was dimly lit with a large round table in the middle. The children were all sitting on one side of the table.

"I win!" exclaimed Neil. "Again!"

"How do you do it?" asked Charlie, tossing a couple of quarters over to Neil.

"He cheats, probably," said Kate, also throwing a few coins in Neil's direction.

"How about another game?" asked Neil, ignoring Kate's remark. "Shall we up the stakes a little? I'll raise you a dollar."

"Ooh, big money!" said Charlie as he threw a few more quarters into the middle of the table.

"A dollar it is," said Kate as she did the same. The teenagers continued their game until about nine o'clock. By this time, Charlie decided that he had lost quite enough money to Neil and wanted to add more to his short story. He decided to write at the window seat in the dining room.

In the card game, the tables had turned and Kate had just won fifty cents back from Neil. Charlie laughed and then leaned back against the window and thought for a while. After chewing on his pen for a minute, he began writing. He wrote for an hour until ten o'clock when he was halfway through the second part of the series.

Kate and Neil were packing up the cards and Charlie flipped the page on his notebook over to reveal a new sheet of blank paper. He took the notebook upstairs and set it on his bedside table again before taking a shower and getting into bed. Within minutes, he was asleep.

📖　　　📖　　　📖

Suddenly, Charlie awoke with a start. He was in a dark room, and he felt trapped. The door to the room was almost fully bricked up. A face glanced into the room and laughed before placing another brick onto the wall, completely blocking the door. The last shaft of flickering light—perhaps candlelight—disappeared. He was alone in the dark. He tried calling for help, but his voice was muffled by the walls. He called again and again. He began to panic as his heart beat faster and faster. He stood up and staggered forward. He walked into a wall and rebounded off it, then became disoriented as he staggered around the room. He hit a corner and staggered backwards. He found another wall and started to beat against the stone, then he began to scramble and tried to dig his way through with his fingernails while

screaming to be let out. Charlie became dizzy as the air in the room grew stale and the oxygen ran out. He was slowly beginning to suffocate! Charlie stepped back and stopped screaming before suddenly collapsing to the floor. He barely felt himself hit the ground. Before Charlie completely lost consciousness, he heard demonic laughter echoing in the distance. Then his body went limp and Charlie lay unconscious on the floor as he slowly suffocated.

■   ■   ■

Charlie sat up with a start. The weak autumn sun was shining through the window and he realized he was in his bed. He was drenched in a cold sweat and the bed sheets were tightly entwined around his body. He relaxed and sighed—it was only a dream.

Charlie remembered the dream and shuddered. It had seemed so real. The feeling of claustrophobia he had felt in the dream came back briefly. It soon subsided and Charlie began wondering what to do that day.

The dream completely forgotten, Charlie got up and got dressed. He picked up his watch from his bedside table next to the notebook with half a page of his neat writing on it. Charlie then went downstairs and made himself a quick breakfast before going into the living room to watch TV. He found Neil in there, sitting on the floor.

"Good morning, Neil," greeted Charlie.

"Morning," replied Neil chewing his thumbnail.

"What are you watching?" asked Charlie.

"Just the usual cartoons," said Neil. Neil stood up and settled himself onto the couch before picking at his thumb again.

They watched TV together for half an hour before Mom came down and asked Charlie and Neil to get some groceries from the nearby store.

The boys stood up and immediately began making their way down the worn road.

"How's the story going?" asked Neil casually as the boys walked side-by-side down the street.

"Fine," said Charlie vacantly. The boys stepped into the grass to let a car go by and Neil looked at Charlie's face. He saw that Charlie wasn't really concentrating on what he was saying.

"What are you thinking about?" asked Neil.

"Oh nothing—just a dream," replied Charlie shaking his head as if to remove the memories of the dream.

Five minutes later they reached the store and went in. They had never been to this store before they had moved because it had been on the other side of town.

The store was very old fashioned. Instead of the bright fluorescent lights found in most modern stores, there was a solitary bulb hanging from the ceiling. The shelves were stacked with cans of food made by little-known manufacturers. All of the shelves had a thick layer of dust, indicating not just that no one cleaned the place very often but that they didn't seem to have much success at selling anything either. At the counter, which was next to the door, there was a cash register and a couple of charity boxes. There was no one at the register, but behind the string curtain there was the sound of whistling. Charlie picked up a rusting basket and the boys began searching for the items from the list their mom had given them. They had nearly finished gathering everything when suddenly there was a triumphant cry from the counter.

"Hah! I told 'em! I told 'em! But would they listen? Would they ever! I've got you young ruffians! I know you're stealing from me! I've got you this time!" An old man had come from behind the curtain and was pointing a shaking finger at the boys.

"Actually, we're buying this stuff," said Charlie, gesturing with his wallet. "Unlikely as it may seem," he muttered under his breath, looking at a suspiciously rusty can of tuna.

"Yeah, sure," said the old man settling back into a chair behind the counter.

Charlie and Neil hurriedly finished finding the last items on the list and then went to the counter. The old man charged Charlie accordingly, hit the lever on the old fashioned cash register, and scraped out the change for the boys.

"I ain't seen ya 'ere before," said the old man. "You new?"

"We moved from the other side of town," replied Neil.

"I take that as a 'yes,'" grumbled the old man. "Where ya moved to? Somewhere nearby?"

"Into the empty house on Two Oaks Road," said Neil before Charlie could stop him.

"Haaa-haaaaa-haaaaa!" laughed the old man suddenly. "You've moved into the 'aunted 'ouse!"

"What do you mean?" asked Charlie.

"I mean what I say." The man grinned. "That

'ouse is 'aunted."

"Oh! Haunted house," said Charlie with a laugh. "You mean haunted house."

"Yeah, that's right—'aunted 'ouse."

"I don't believe in ghosts," said Charlie.

"That's what they all say," said the old man with a sinister smile, "before it 'appens."

"Before what 'appens—I mean, happens?" demanded Neil.

"You'll see," replied the old man. "You'll see."

With that, the old man turned abruptly and went back through the bead curtain laughing.

"Before what happens?" asked Neil again, half to himself.

"Nothing—he's just trying to scare us, that's all," said Charlie, as he led the way out of the shop. "The guy must enjoy scaring local kids."

"Mean-spirited old man," spat Neil.

"He probably gets bored working in that smelly shop," said Charlie, trying to be fair.

"Yeah, it did stink," answered Neil as they began to walk up the hill toward the house.

The boys entered the house at half past nine, and everyone was awake. Kate had just finished eating breakfast and was watching TV. She looked up as Charlie and Neil entered the living room having just dropped the groceries off in the kitchen.

"Hi," she greeted.

"Hi, Kate," replied Charlie.

"Yeah, hi," said Neil.

"What do we wanna do today?" asked Kate.

"How about searching the attic for anything left here from the people before us," suggested Charlie.

"Okay," agreed Kate.

"All right," said Neil.

The teenagers were up in the attic in no time at all. It was basically empty except for three old boxes in one corner. Charlie opened the first box. It was wooden and revealed nothing but a small pile of old sawdust. Charlie moved over to the next one and lifted the lid. The result was the same—just a small pile of sawdust.

Disheartened, Charlie began to lift the lid of the last and smallest box. The lid shifted and then stuck. Charlie tugged the lid again but the lid still refused to move. Charlie changed his grip on it and tried again. Suddenly the lid shot open and Charlie staggered back.

"Ow!" he cried as blood began to seep through a deep gash in his left hand. Charlie looked down at the box and saw that he must have caught his hand on a nail protruding from the side. He put his hand into his mouth and sucked it.

"Are you okay?" asked Kate.

"I'm fine. What's in the box?"

"Nothing—no, there is something—a book." Kate bent over and picked the box up from where it had been half concealed by bits of sawdust.

"What's in it?" asked Neil.

"Nothing. It's a diary but there are no entries.

Wait, there is one, here on the 15th of November."

"That's today," interrupted Neil.

"It says," continued Kate, glancing up at Neil, "'Charles, help me. I need help!'"

"Is that it?" asked Charlie, taking the book from Kate's hands.

"Yeah," replied Kate. "What a coincidence that it happened to be today's date."

"And it says 'Charles' in it," said Neil.

"I wonder why he needed help?" said Charlie vacantly.

"Why 'he'?" demanded Kate.

"I don't know," replied Charlie with a shrug.

"If that's all that's up here we should go back down now?" asked Neil.

"Yeah," answered Charlie. "There's nothing else up here that's interesting."

Charlie, Kate, and Neil didn't do much for the rest of the day. They mostly just messed around and played video games and cards. By the evening, Charlie couldn't be bothered to write, so he just read the story through from the beginning to check for mistakes. He was sitting in the dining room with Kate and Neil. He read a piece of the story which he wasn't sure about, so he stood up from the window seat and went over to Kate to ask her opinion. After she had given him her opinion, Charlie sat down next to her. He continued reading, occasionally turning a page. He stopped reading for a moment to think for a bit. He half-listened to Kate and Neil playing cards and looked around the dining room. He saw the old antique bookcases, which had been in the house when they had arrived, the old sideboard that they had brought from their previous house, and the window seat with a depression in the middle of the padded fabric, which he assumed had occurred from many years of use.

He went back to reading his story again and

flipped the page. Charlie frowned and flipped the page back again. He rubbed the page between his fingers to see if he'd turned two pages.

Charlie shrugged and continued reading.

He sat back and took in his surroundings—the bookcases, the sideboard, the window seat. The two other figures were hunched over the table playing cards. One cried out triumphantly and pulled his winnings toward him. He then glanced back at the window seat to see a shadowy figure was sitting there, quietly smiling to himself. The person had been there longer than anyone could remember, and he always sat at the window smiling to himself.

Suddenly Charlie's eyes glazed over and he reeled back from the notebook. He hadn't written this—it was in his handwriting, yes, but it wasn't written with a ballpoint pen.

Charlie slowly glanced up at the window.

A shadowy figure half raised its hand in acknowledgment. Charlie could just make out a smile beneath the dark shadow of the flat cap the figure wore.

"Neil, Kate…" began Charlie, his voice quivering.

"What, Charlie?" asked Kate. She looked in the direction of Charlie's frightened gaze and frowned. "What? Did you see something outside?"

Charlie blinked and saw only the window and the seat. "G-g-g-gho—" stammered Charlie.

"Go where?" asked Kate nervously looking back to the window again.

Charlie shook his head as if trying to clear a thought.

"What's up Charlie? You look like you've seen a ghost," said Neil.

"I think I just did," said Charlie in a suddenly calm voice.

CHAPTER THREE

The Room

Charlie showed Kate and Neil the notebook with the new writing in it.

"I finished at the bottom of the last page," said Charlie, "but look—suddenly there's this extra writing saying exactly what I was doing in the dining room. Come to think of it, I noticed that extra writing this morning, but I didn't really think about it until now."

"Yeah right, Charlie," sneered Neil.

"It's true!" maintained Charlie.

"You could have written it in the dining room, Charlie," said Kate doubtfully. "There's no such thing as ghosts. You've got us all scared but you're taking this prank a little too far."

"It's not a prank!" insisted Charlie.

"Sure, Charlie," said Neil in a patronizing voice guaranteed to start a brotherly fight.

"Why don't you believe me?!" pleaded Charlie miserably.

"Because it all sounds a little far-fetched," said Kate kindly. "I think we should just forget it—you were probably just imagining things." She threw a warning look across the table to Neil who was just about to say something else. He took the hint and decided to stay tight-lipped.

"What about the story then?" demanded Charlie.

"You probably did it earlier and forgot about it," replied Kate sensibly.

Charlie sighed and then relented, "Yeah, that's probably it."

"Hi, kids!" shouted Dad as he suddenly came into the room. Dad tossed three bars of chocolate onto the table in front of the three of them.

"Snacks! Let's watch a movie," he explained.

As they exited the room to go to the living room, Charlie—who was the last out—looked back toward the window. A shadowy figure waved at him from the window seat and winked. Charlie hurried out and slammed the door behind him. Once on the other side of the door he shivered then quickly followed the rest of the family into the living room to watch the movie. It was a scary movie they all had been dying to watch. Charlie wasn't at all surprised.

After what had happened in the last few minutes, Charlie didn't find the movie the least bit scary. Afterwards, he thought about the shadowy figure on the window seat and decided that he must have imagined it. But he still couldn't figure out how the extra writing had appeared on his notebook.

Having rekindled the fear he had earlier, he was

reluctant to go to bed. As it was vacation and Mom and Dad didn't mind what time he went to bed, he asked Kate and Neil if they wanted to stay up and play cards or a board game.

Kate and Neil guessed the reason why he wanted to stay up but they didn't say anything, partly because Charlie and the movie had unnerved them enough to want to return to a sense of normalcy.

They decided on Monopoly. Neil was the best at Monopoly and always won. No one had ever beaten him at it ever since he had started playing. Charlie and Kate always tried to gang up on him when they played but to no avail. Charlie was only glad that they didn't play with real money. Neil, however, was not.

After an hour or two of intense Monopoly playing, Neil emerged victorious. Charlie and Kate weren't at all surprised. The teenagers were in much higher spirits now and happily went to bed having forgotten what had happened earlier on. Charlie wearily set his notebook on his bedside table out of habit and slid beneath the cool covers.

Suddenly Charlie awoke. He was in the room again, only this time the doorway was only half bricked up. The same face looked over the bricks and laughed at Charlie lying on the floor. The face was easier to make out this time. Charlie could see a beard now among the darkened features.

Charlie tried to stand up and escape but he couldn't will his body to move. The face looked at Charlie again and grinned.

"So you're awake now, you dirty piece of slime," the figure said suddenly while looking directly at Charlie. "This'll teach you."

Charlie tried to stand up again, this time gaining some momentum. He began writhing on the floor, but that was the most he could bring himself to do. He accidentally hit his head against the rough stone floor and became unconscious.

Charlie awoke again with a start. He was still in the room. The door to the room was almost fully bricked up. Charlie could see the cement oozing between the bricks. The face glanced into the room again and laughed maniacally before placing another brick onto the wall blocking up the doorway. Soon the last brick went in and the last shaft of flickering light—probably candle or lamplight—disappeared, and he was alone in the dark. He started calling for help, but his voice was muffled by the stone walls. He called again and again. He began to panic as his heart beat faster and faster. He stood up and staggered forward. He hit a wall and rebounded off it. He became disoriented as he staggered around the room. He felt as though he were falling. He hit a corner and staggered backwards. He found another wall and started to beat against the stone, crying for help. Then he began to scramble and tried to dig his way through with his fingernails while screaming to be let out. Charlie became dizzy as the air in the room grew stale and the oxygen ran out. He was slowly beginning to suffocate. Charlie stepped back and stopped screaming before suddenly collapsing to the floor. Before Charlie completely lost consciousness, he heard demonic laughter echoing in the distance. Then his body went limp and Charlie lay unconscious on the floor as he slowly suffocated.

CHAPTER FOUR

The Man on the Window Seat

The bright morning light sparkled through Charlie's window and Charlie turned over to try to shield his eyes from it. As he awoke, he remembered the dream. This time there had been more—only a little, but still more. This morning the sheets had again become knotted around his body, as if he had been moving in his sleep, and they were wet from Charlie's sweat.

Charlie felt a chill run down his spine and hoped that he wouldn't dream the dream again tonight. With a conscious effort not to look at his notebook, Charlie got out of bed and got dressed. He remembered the night before and shuddered.

That guy at the store yesterday was right, he thought, this house is haunted.

Charlie went into the bathroom wearily and washed his face. He rubbed his eyes and looked at himself in the mirror blearily. There were heavy bags under his eyes, evidence of his lack of sleep. He decided to go to bed early tonight.

Charlie slowly got dressed and went downstairs to the kitchen where Kate was finishing her cereal.

"Wow, Charlie, you look awful," she remarked.

"I feel awful. How come you're not tired?" Charlie asked.

"Because we didn't go to bed that late last night," replied Kate.

Charlie thought back for a few seconds and frowned. "You're right. I didn't go to bed that late either, so why am I so tired?"

"Beats me," answered Kate shrugging. "Maybe you should go back to sleep."

"No, I'm too awake now," said Charlie.

"You don't look very awake," commented Kate.

"Hi, people!" greeted Neil, before looking at Charlie's face and saying, "You look terrible."

"Good morning to you too," said Charlie in a deadpan voice.

"What were you up to last night?" asked Neil.

"Nothing," said Charlie.

"Are you sure?" Neil asked.

"Well," began Charlie, "there was one thing that happened. I had this dream two nights ago that I had again last night. The funny thing was that last night the dream was a little longer—there was more at the beginning."

"What happened in the dream?" asked Neil.

"Give me a few minutes and I'll tell you," said Charlie as he sat down at the kitchen table and rested his hands on its mottled surface.

Charlie told his brother and sister about the dream and the dark room and the bricked up doorway and the bearded face and the feeling of claustrophobia and passing out and waking up with his bed sheets twisted around his body.

"Have you ever had a dream like this before?" asked Kate.

"No, I haven't," replied Charlie. "They only started when we moved here."

Suddenly a look of revelation come across Neil's face and he turned to Charlie.

"Did the bearded guy look anything like the shadowy guy last night on the window seat?" he asked Charlie rapidly.

Charlie thought about this for a second and then shook his head.

"No, from what I saw, the shadowy figure on the window seat didn't have a beard," he answered.

"I wonder why you only began dreaming this dream when we arrived here," said Kate.

"I don't know," said Charlie. "But if I dream it tonight then dreaming the same thing twice was no coincidence."

The teenagers were quiet for a while until Charlie said, "Speaking of the man at the window seat..."

"Go on..." said Neil.

"Well when we went into the living room I was the last one out and I saw the figure again. It waved to me."

"Suddenly I really don't feel like believing you anymore," said Neil.

"Just wait," said Charlie. "Every morning since we moved here, there has been extra writing in my notebook that I never wrote. Now unless one of you is playing a practical joke on me, I don't know how it got there."

"Can I see your notebook?" asked Kate.

"Sure," said Charlie standing up. "I'll go get it."

When Charlie returned, he placed the notebook on the table and turned to the latest page.

"Look! More writing," he pointed out, "and it's different—it's that ink stuff, not ballpoint."

"You're right, the ink is different," said Neil.

Charlie read the new words out loud.

The man awoke and stretched. He had fallen asleep on the window seat again while writing his latest book. Suddenly, the man recollected what he had to do and sighed. For many years he had been good friends with the person he was about to report to the local policeman. They had gone to school together. But what his friend had done was too terrible to ignore—too terrible, indeed.

"Are you sure you didn't write this?" asked Kate.

"Look, I'd know if I wrote something or not, wouldn't I?" said Charlie defensively. "I don't know who's doing this but I want it to stop."

"So what should we do?" answered Kate.

"Go into the dining room and watch the man from the story wake up," he sighed.

The children went into the dining room apprehensively to see if the writing was going to become a reality. Kate and Neil still didn't quite believe Charlie, but for some reason, the way he was acting about the whole thing unnerved them and they were beginning to get sucked into a situation they weren't completely sure they'd be able to get out of.

Charlie flung the door open as he entered the room. The door hit the wall, bounced back and rebounded off Charlie's shoe.

He barely noticed the door hitting his shoe as he looked across the room toward the large bay window. On the window seat in the shadow of an almighty oak was the figure that Charlie had seen the night before. The figure wore a flat cap and the teenagers could just about make out the crisscross pattern on the figure's tweed jacket. The figure—a man—sat on the seat with his back resting against the side of the bay window. His head was slumped forward against his knees which were hunched up against his body. The man was obviously sleeping.

The teenagers could not make out the man's face, as it was hidden half by his flat cap and half by his knees. Suddenly the man moved. He grunted slightly and sat back. The teenagers could make out grey-streaked, greasy, brown hair sticking out at crazy angles from beneath his hat. The teenagers could also smell a faint hint of boiled cabbage.

Charlie seemed to pull himself together and stepped forward. "Who are you? What do you want?" he demanded in sudden anger.

The man ignored him.

"Charlie!" shouted Mom from upstairs suddenly. "Why are you yelling?"

Kate and Neil briefly turned and looked in the direction of Mom's voice.

"Nothing, Mom!" Charlie called back, turning around slightly.

"Okay. Well try to keep it down please."

"Okay, Mom!" Charlie replied.

He turned back at the same moment as Kate

and Neil and staggered back in shock. The man was gone. Charlie rushed over to the window seat in astonishment and stood there speechless, looking for the man. But he was gone.

All that was left was the faint smell of boiled cabbage.

"Where is he?" Charlie almost wailed.

He had been sitting with his brother and sister at the dining room table and looking in the direction of the window seat for an hour.

"He couldn't have just vanished," said Neil unhelpfully.

"Well he did," said Kate, her voice still quivering slightly. "But what I want to know is how did he get there?"

"Well at least him being there proved I'm not a liar," said Charlie triumphantly, having finally snapped out of the trance he had been in.

"You might be right about a man being there,

but it could be possible that this guy broke in, fiddled with your notebook, and then waited until we read it and came in to the dining room," Kate said in a matter-of-fact voice.

"Come on, Kate, you don't actually believe that, do you? You think he quietly opened the bay window, which actually doesn't open, snuck upstairs, wrote some stuff in my notebook with a fountain pen he just happened to bring along with him in exactly the same handwriting as my own, then snuck downstairs into the dining room until morning in the hope that nobody would go in there until after they had read my notebook, and then waited for a chance to leap out of the window, which still doesn't open, and then very quietly closed it again when we all just happened to look away! No way!"

Kate couldn't say anything for a second or two after Charlie's sudden outburst, but she defended herself weakly by demanding, "Well what do you think happened?"

She instantly regretted saying that as Charlie got even more furious.

"I don't know! But I am going to find out!" he replied, emphasizing each word he spoke. Kate stayed quiet then, as she knew she couldn't say anything else to improve the situation. She was shocked at Charlie's outburst—he was normally the one who stayed calm all the time and rarely got annoyed. On the rare occasions he did get annoyed, he was never this bad and he always cracked up laughing afterward. Something really must be getting to him, she thought. But what? It must be this house. I'm beginning to hate it more and more as these freaky things keep happening.

CHAPTER FIVE

Someone Wants Me Dead

The teenagers spent the rest of the day by themselves. They didn't really feel like talking to each other after what had happened. Charlie stayed in his bedroom at his desk, thinking and occasionally scribbling things down on a scrap of paper. Kate read a book in her room, and Neil played a video game in the living room. Mom and Dad had gone out and wouldn't be back until later on in the evening.

At about five o'clock, Charlie stood up, shoved the scrap of paper he was writing on into his pocket and walked downstairs to the kitchen. About five minutes later, Neil got up from the sofa. Then he too went into the kitchen. He met Kate just inside the door. They glanced at each other but didn't say anything and then they both walked toward the table. Charlie was sitting there reading a cardboard flyer advertising a local takeout pizza restaurant. He looked up and smiled weakly.

"Anyone want pizza?" he asked awkwardly. After spending a day in silence it felt strange to hear someone talking and Charlie's voice sounded hollow and seemed to echo off the bare stone walls.

"Yeah, I wouldn't mind some pizza," answered Neil in a slightly croaky voice. He cleared his throat. "I'm starving."

"Me too," added Kate.

Suddenly it seemed as if a barrier had been broken. The teenagers relaxed and felt able to talk easily again.

"I wonder what's on TV," said Neil. "That new series should be on tonight. You know, the one about the aliens."

"Oh yeah, I know what you're talking about. What's it called again?" replied Charlie.

"If you two want to watch your childish shows, I guess I have no choice but to watch them with you," sighed Kate.

"Should I go ahead and order the pizza now?" asked Charlie.

"Hang on a second, what are you ordering?" asked Neil indignantly. "Don't we get a choice?"

"No," replied Charlie picking up the phone and pretending to dial the number. He laughed as Neil launched himself at him and Charlie held the phone out of Neil's reach. Neil climbed himself up Charlie and made a grab for the phone.

"Okay! Okay!" laughed Charlie, pushing Neil out of the way. "I haven't actually called yet. What do you want?"

"Pepperoni with extra cheese!" cried Neil.

"Me too," said Kate.

"Okay, I can live with that," said Charlie while

dialing the pizza delivery number. Suddenly his face went white and he dropped the phone and stood rooted to the spot, staring at nothing.

"What's wrong Charlie?" asked Kate in concern.

"He doesn't look okay," said Neil. He picked up the phone, which had cracked when it had hit the floor and put it to his ear. He frowned. "There's no one there—there's just static on the other end."

"Charlie? What did they say?" asked Kate frantically shaking him at the same time. Charlie just swayed slightly. Kate pushed him gently onto a chair and said to Neil, "I've never seen him like this before!" She looked back at Charlie and again asked, "What did they say?"

Charlie blinked once or twice and shook his head. The color slowly came back to his cheeks and he said, "Someone wants me dead," in a flat and monotonous voice.

"What?!" demanded Neil.

"Someone—a man, I think—said to me,

'Charlie, if you stick your nose into anything that doesn't concern you, you won't live to see the next day. The same goes if you tell anyone else.'"

"What did he mean?" asked Kate.

"I think I know," began Neil.

"The voice," interrupted Charlie, "sounded familiar, as if I'd heard it somewhere before."

"Think, Charlie. Who was it?" asked Kate.

"I don't know!" wailed Charlie. "But I know what the guy meant!"

"So do I," said Neil.

"What did he mean?" demanded Kate.

"You mean you don't know?" asked Charlie.

"No, I don't," replied Kate. "Unless you mean…" she looked into Charlie's eyes, and he nodded.

"Yes, I do."

"Neil?" she asked, looking at Neil.

"I agree," said Neil.

"But that's crazy!" she cried, "There's no such thing as—" she paused.

"Go on—say it," urged Charlie.

"Ghosts," she muttered.

"Oh, come on, Kate, wake up and smell the coffee! You've seen the evidence! That man in the dining room—he wasn't a real person—he disappeared!"

"Also there was the diary in the attic. Someone needs help," said Neil.

"I think," said Charlie, "and this is a long shot, but I think that someone else was killed here and someone doesn't want us finding out."

Kate looked into Charlie's eyes and saw pure conviction in them.

"I agree," said Neil, "I think that we should find out who."

"But what about Charlie's threat?" asked Kate.

"I'll be fine," said Charlie. "Don't worry."

Kate and Neil knew that Charlie was scared for his life, but that wasn't going to stop him. All they could do was follow him and help.

CHAPTER SIX

The Missing Man

Charlie was sitting on the window seat and looking out the window at the oak tree. The oak tree was quite young and barely grew to the height of the second floor of the house. A shadow fell over him from behind. Charlie began to turn around when suddenly someone struck him with a crushing blow to the head and Charlie blacked out.

Charlie awoke. He was in the darkened room again, only this time the doorway was only half bricked up. Charlie could make out a dark square object behind the bearded figure bricking him into the room. The bearded face looked over the bricks and laughed at Charlie lying on the floor. Charlie tried to stand up and escape but he couldn't will his body to move. The face looked at Charlie again and grinned.

"So you're awake now, you dirty piece of slime," the figure said suddenly, looking directly at Charlie. "This'll teach you."

The face grinned horribly. Charlie tried to stand up again, but he could only writhe about helplessly. He hit his head against the rough stone floor and became unconscious.

Suddenly Charlie awoke with a start. He was still in the room. The door to the room was almost fully bricked up. The face glanced smugly into the room again and laughed before placing another brick onto the wall blocking up the door. Soon the last brick went in and the last shaft of flickering candle or lamplight disappeared and he was alone in the dark.

He started calling for help, but his voice was muffled by the stone walls. He called over and over.

He began to panic as his heart went into overdrive. He stood up and staggered forward. He hit a cold, hard wall and rebounded off it. He became disoriented as he staggered around the room, flailing his arms. He hit a corner and staggered backwards, out of control. He found another wall and started to beat against the stone, then he began to scramble and tried to dig his way through with his fingernails while screaming to be let out. Charlie began to become dizzy as the air in the room grew stale and the oxygen ran out. He was slowly beginning to suffocate. Charlie stepped back and stopped screaming before suddenly collapsing to the floor. Before Charlie completely lost consciousness, he heard demonic laughter echoing in the distance. Then his body went limp and Charlie lay unconscious on the floor as he slowly suffocated.

Tap-tap-tap. Tap-tap-tap. Tap-tap-tap.

Charlie opened his eyes and scanned the room for the source of the noise. The door? No. The wardrobe? No. The window?

Tap-tap-tap went the oak's branch, banging against the window as the tree was shaken by the wind. The wind blowing through the leaves made a shrill whistling sound as if a thousand ghosts were screaming in torment. Charlie shivered as he remembered the dream.

It was strange, he pondered, the dream felt so real that he didn't realize it was only a dream.

"Now, what was new?" he muttered to himself. "The window seat—I was sitting there looking at the tree." He glanced up at the branches which were still tapping the window. "And suddenly a person hit me over the head."

Charlie shook his head in exasperation and climbed out of his bed. The house was comfortably warm when Charlie tiptoed over the soft carpet to the bathroom.

After taking a hot shower, Charlie filled his siblings in on his dream.

"I wonder what will happen next," said Kate.

"I don't know, but I will next time I go to sleep," answered Charlie.

"Where should we begin investigating your theory about a 'murder' in the house, Charlie?" asked Neil.

"The computer, of course," replied Charlie.

Charlie typed in "murder" on a local newspaper archive website on the family computer. Fifty articles came up, but they were unrelated to their house.

"Try searching 'missing' instead," suggested Kate.

"Okay," said Charlie, typing the word in the search box. One hundred and sixty articles.

"This is hopeless," said Neil. "Can't we narrow it down a bit?"

"We could if we knew any dates," said Charlie. "Hang on! I've got it!"

"What?" asked Kate.

"The oak tree in my dream didn't reach my bedroom window by a few feet, but this morning I woke up to the sound of one of its branches tapping my window!"

"That must put it back to a little over one hundred years ago," said Neil.

"Great!" exclaimed Charlie.

He specified dates between 1900 and 1920 and sat back to watch the results come up.

"There are thirty articles with the word 'missing' in them," said Charlie.

"Which ones are on our street?" asked Kate.

Charlie narrowed the search. "There are five," said Charlie. "Three are about missing children who ran away from home, another is a missing woman, and the last is a missing man."

"The man lived in our house! Look at the address!" cried Kate suddenly, after reading the screen over Charlie's shoulder, "I don't believe it, but it's true!"

Charlie was shocked. "The guy who went missing was a forty-nine-year-old teacher," he said. "One day he didn't turn up at the school and never returned. People searched his house but found no sign of him. He seemed to have disappeared."

"Perhaps he was bricked in a room in the house like in your dream?" suggested Kate.

"But wouldn't someone have noticed a bricked up room?" asked Neil.

"The article says that he led a solitary lifestyle," replied Charlie. "Anyone searching his house may not have noticed a missing room."

"But what about the new bricks and fresh concrete?" Neil continued.

"The murderer could have painted over the bricks or put up a wooden panel to cover up the brickwork," Charlie answered.

"I think that we should search the house for any old rooms," stated Kate. "But how should we go about it?"

"Let's just search downstairs," said Charlie.

"Why?" asked Neil.

"Because," answered Charlie, "the teacher guy was bricked into a room that had a stone floor."

"Oh yeah," said Neil, slapping his forehead.

"Anyway, we should go around the house tapping the wooden walls and listening for a thud instead of a hollow sound to indicate a brick wall behind them. Then we can…"

"We could take a panel down carefully," suggested Neil.

"That's true," replied Charlie. "If we don't find anything suspicious after we have tapped all the panels in the house, we can then look for irregular brickwork—maybe in the shape of a doorway."

"I think we should do that first," said Kate.

"You're right, Kate," said Charlie. "That'll be easier to look out for."

"What if we don't find anything?" asked Neil.

"We'll have to keep looking," replied Charlie.

"When should we start our search?" asked Kate.

"Right now" Charlie replied, his voice suddenly sounding cold. "I'm determined to figure this out, even if it kills me."

The children went silent. As they suddenly remembered the voice from the night before on the telephone, they had a chilling thought that Charlie's words might come back to haunt him.

They started in the kitchen and began examining the walls intently. It took them about ten minutes and they found nothing. They searched the dining room and the living room but they did not find any irregular brickwork there.

"This is hopeless," said Neil despondently.

"We're just getting started," said Charlie attempting to lift the mood. "We still have to search the wooden walls."

"I'm beginning to wonder if there isn't a ghost

after all," Kate sighed.

"Look," began Charlie, "I've told you, this is no wild goose chase."

"Do you really think that?" asked Neil.

"Yes!" answered Charlie. "I absolutely do!"

The teenagers spent the next hour examining every wall in the house with no success.

They were in Dad's study and were searching the last wall.

"Hang on," cried Charlie. "I think I've got it!" His triumphant grin fell as he realized it wasn't the correct wall after all—it was another outside wall.

He sat down and rested his chin on his fist.

"I don't get it," he sighed. "We've looked everywhere and still haven't found anything!"

Kate sat across from him and also sighed.

"I really thought we were onto something," she said, "but it turns out there's nothing."

"Hey! I've got it!" Neil cried. "I've got it!"

"What, Neil?" asked Charlie wearily.

"I know what we've missed!" Neil shouted.

"Which is?" Kate asked him.

"We forgot to look behind furniture!"

Charlie and Kate looked at each other in disbelief.

"Of course!" Charlie exclaimed. "Good thinking, Neil. We should check all the furniture!"

"Let's go!" said Kate.

After pulling an antique stack of shelves carefully away from the wall, the teenagers found what they were looking for.

"It must have been the old pantry," Charlie decided.

"I wonder who put the teacher guy in there," said Kate.

"From what I remember the murderer had a beard and a slender, pale face."

"What kind of beard?" asked Neil.

"Like Abraham Lincoln," Charlie said.

"That could have been anyone," sighed Kate.

"Maybe my next dream will tell me who it was," said Charlie.

"Maybe," said Neil dubiously.

"It's funny though," said Charlie, as he helped Neil put the stack of shelves back.

"What is?" asked Neil.

"The voice on the phone—it was so familiar, yet I can't put a finger on it."

That night the teenagers watched television until eleven o'clock before going to bed. Charlie felt apprehensive as he slipped beneath the covers and it was a long time before he went to sleep.

CHAPTER SEVEN

The Hooded Figures

Charlie awoke. He was crouching in a dimly lit room looking over some sort of desk. He could hear chanting. Charlie went onto his hands and knees and crawled to the edge of the desk and peered around. He saw nothing, only flickering light. Charlie could smell some sort of incense. It wafted up his nostrils and became chokingly thick. Charlie began to feel dizzy and shook his head to get rid of the feeling. He then crept to the next corner of the desk and peered around it. Five shadowy, hooded figures were standing at each point of a five-sided star. Each held a candle and chanted something in a language Charlie couldn't

understand. He wondered if it was Latin.

The figures were focused on the star intently. Suddenly a sixth figure entered the room and stood before a podium and began chanting. The figure's hood fell, revealing a man's face with a Lincoln beard. The man's teeth were showing, tightly gripped together behind thin, curled lips.

Charlie poked his head around the desk and watched in terror and amazement as a red mist seemed to be sucking toward the center of the star where it became a twisting column that spun like a miniature whirlwind. The mist lit the faces of the chanters but not the bearded man. He had put the hood back over his head, but Charlie could still distinctly see two yellow ovals beneath the hood. The man began chanting something different from the others. His voice became deep and otherworldly—almost like a demon. The man's voice became louder and louder and more and more distorted until Charlie couldn't believe it was still a man speaking.

Suddenly the man looked at one of the figures on one corner of the star and said in an evil voice, "You don't truuuuly belieeeve."

The robed chanter stammered and said in a meek voice, "I d-do."

"BEGONE!" shouted the man whom Charlie decided had to be the leader.

Two orange and flaming beams of light from the leader's yellow, glowing eyes tore across the room and hit the disbeliever at his feet. The beams swept slowly up the person's body, vaporizing it as it went, until only the robe remained.

The bearded figure laughed at the empty robe and said, "Let this be a lesson to you all! Now leave! And remember not to leave anything behind, or you will suffer immensely."

The figure suddenly stopped in the process of leaving and said, "May I remind you not to tell anyone what happened here tonight, unless you want your spirit to live in torment forever!"

Charlie felt as if the person was talking to him directly and shuddered.

Ten minutes later, all of the shadowy figures had left, the last having blown the candles out.

For the next few minutes Charlie sat in darkness until he felt sure that it was safe to leave. He wondered where he was as he quickly opened the nearest window and climbed out onto the ground floor. He crept from the building and looked for a way home. The area seemed familiar. Suddenly, he realized it was his school! The new building wasn't there but the old one was the same as it had always been. The teacher must have discovered the evil magic that was being practiced by these people and was going to report it. One of the people must have killed him before he had a chance to. So the bearded man must have been talking to me, Charlie decided. The man had the same voice as the phone voice and also looked the same as the murderer, Charlie thought.

Charlie sighed as he made his way back to the house under the full moon, unhappy in the knowledge of what would happen next. When he got in, he went straight to the dining room to sit down and think. The dining room was dark, so he found a flashlight and set it up beside him. Before long he had dozed off into dreamless sleep.

Charlie awoke again. He was still sitting at the window seat. He looked out of the window at the oak tree. The oak tree was quite young and barely grew to the height of the second floor of the house. A shadow fell over him from behind. Charlie knew who it was but still began to turn around to see the person. Suddenly the person struck him with a crushing blow to the head and Charlie blacked out.

Charlie awoke. He was in the darkened room again. The doorway was half bricked up. Charlie tried to make out the dark square object behind the bearded figure bricking him in and realized that it was the shelf. The bearded face looked over the bricks and laughed at Charlie lying on the floor. Charlie tried to stand up and escape, but he couldn't will his body to move. He felt as though he had been drugged. The face looked at Charlie again and grinned.

"So you're awake now, you dirty piece of slime," the owner of the face sneered, looking at Charlie. "This'll teach you."

The owner of the face was the same person from earlier at the school.

Charlie tried to stand up again, this time gaining some momentum. He began writhing on the floor, but that was the most he could do. He hit his head against the rough stone floor and became unconscious.

Suddenly, Charlie awoke with a start. He was still in the room. By now he knew exactly what to expect. Charlie sighed reluctantly at the thought of going through the same thing all over again.

CHAPTER EIGHT

I Am Right!

Charlie sat up, suddenly wide awake. He looked around and saw that he was in his bedroom. Charlie tensed as he remembered his nightmare.

Charlie shivered and then climbed out of bed. He went into the bathroom to take a quick shower before having breakfast downstairs in the kitchen.

"Good morning, Charlie!" greeted Kate, coming into the kitchen. She saw the pallid look on Charlie's face and frowned. "What's wrong?"

Charlie looked at her and Kate suddenly knew what was wrong.

"The dream?" she asked.

"Yeah," he replied sullenly.

"What happened?" Kate asked inquisitively.

"Just give me a few more minutes."

Kate decided not to ask any more questions for the time being and made herself some breakfast. She sat across from Charlie and together they ate in silence. They had both finished when Neil finally came in.

"Morning!" he said cheerfully. He looked at Charlie and sighed. "You had that dream again?"

"Yeah," Charlie sighed back.

"Sorry to hear that," Neil said. "What happened this time?"

Charlie ate his breakfast in silence for a few more minutes before talking.

"It must have been the worst dream I've had in my entire life, and if that was what really happened to this teacher, then we are up against more than your average haunted house," said Charlie.

Kate asked, "It was that bad?"

"Yes, it was pretty bad," he replied. "I'm going

to tell you everything."

Charlie proceeded to tell his brother and sister about the dream. As Charlie spoke, they became more and more horrified.

"You've got to be kidding!" said Neil.

"I'm serious," replied Charlie.

"But it was only a dream," began Kate.

"Which just happens to contain stuff that has really happened so far," retorted Charlie. "So why wouldn't this be true?"

"Well, it sounds made up," said Kate searching for the right words.

"So you believe in ghosts, but not in this other stuff because this other stuff—this 'evil magic'— sounds made up?" Charlie replied hotly.

"Well, as much as I hate to believe him," Neil said, "it looks like we have no choice. Everything else is true, so why not this?"

"Okay, I'll go along with you," Kate sighed, giving in, "but what if you're wrong?"

Charlie looked at her, his eyes burning, and said, "I am right!"

"So what do we do?" asked Neil.

"Let's go to the school and look around," answered Charlie.

"Which room did this ritual happen in?" asked Kate.

"I think it was a math room. Room 84," replied Charlie.

"Have you ever had class in there?" asked Neil.

"Nope. Have you?"

"No," replied Neil.

"Me neither," said Kate shrugging as the boys looked to her for an answer.

"So we know nothing about the room—none of us know anything strange about it," Charlie summarized.

"No, so we should find stuff out about it now," Neil said.

"Right now?" asked Kate.

"Tomorrow. I'm pretty tired," replied Neil.

"But school starts tomorrow," said Kate.

"What should we do, Charlie?" asked Neil. "We're going to be back at school and won't have time to investigate."

"You're forgetting something," said Charlie.

"What?" asked Neil.

"We are going to be at school and can continue our investigation there."

"But what about anything we have to investigate outside of school?"

"Somehow," answered Charlie, "I don't think we are going to be investigating very much outside of school anymore."

CHAPTER NINE

Edward P. Oates

That night Charlie awoke. He was standing at the entrance of the school, holding a big, heavy key in one hand. Charlie inserted the key into the door and turned it. The lock was well oiled and turned silently. Charlie pushed the heavy oak door open and stepped inside. He then quickly made his way along the hallway which led to the math classroom. The hallway was cold and dark. Along one wall were ancient black-and-white photographs of all the school's old principals. Charlie idly looked at each one as he passed them. He recognized most of the photographs, as they were still there today.

Suddenly, Charlie stopped in front of the last

photograph and gasped. The photograph on the wall was that of the bearded man who performed the ritual a few nights ago. Charlie looked at the name on the brass plaque beneath the photograph.

Edward P. Oates 1905-

Charlie memorized this before continuing along the hallway. He entered the room a minute later and went to the desk. On the desk was a folder entitled HOMEWORK. Charlie decided that this was what he must be here for. The teacher had obviously left it behind and had come back for it, only to discover the evil ritual taking place. Charlie hastily picked up the folder, but it fell to the ground, spilling pages all over the floor. Charlie got down onto his knees and had just begun picking all the sheets up when a person wearing a hooded robe slowly walked through the doorway. The figure was quickly followed by another, who was carrying something. Then, four others walked in, each carrying something, and began to set up the things they had brought with them. Candles were set upon tall candle sticks and were lit. One figure drew a precise five-pointed star with chalk onto the floor and then drew a perfect circle around it, which touched each of the five points.

Then the first figure left and the other five stood upon each point of the star and began chanting. They had spoken nothing until now, and Charlie jumped slightly when they began to chant. He put the folder down and sat with his back against the desk. He knew what was going to happen from here, and he didn't like it one bit.

Charlie was awoken by the sound of his alarm clock ringing. Charlie groaned and climbed out of his bed slowly.

Something was nagging him at the edge of his consciousness, but he couldn't quite grasp what. It had something to do with the dream. That was it—he had to remember something. But what?

A name. Ed. Edward. Edward P. Oates! He remembered! What about him, though? The principal with the beard! That was it, he had to remember the name Edward P. Oates from the dream. Edward P. Oates, the principal from 1905.

When had he stopped being a principal? I guess I'll have to find out today, Charlie thought.

Charlie showered and got dressed before having breakfast. He was soon joined by Kate and Neil.

"Morning, Charlie," greeted Neil.

"Good morning," greeted Kate.

"Had that dream again," replied Charlie.

"Was it bad?" inquired Kate, pouring her milk onto her cornflakes.

"The new stuff wasn't, but I re-dreamed that part from last night," Charlie answered.

"Ouch," empathized Neil, "it must be awful dreaming the same terrible thing again and again.

"It is," replied Charlie, "but I found out something new and it's pretty bad."

"What?" Kate asked.

Charlie then told his brother and sister about the photo and the name.

"Do you know what's really strange, though?" Charlie said. "You know I said the bearded guy, Oates, looked familiar."

"Yes," said Neil.

"Well, he still looks familiar, but I can't quite put my finger on why," continued Charlie.

"What do you mean?" asked Kate. "He looked familiar because of the photo on the wall. That must be where you've seen him before."

"That's the thing, I've seen his face somewhere else before but I can't remember where."

Kate and Neil mulled this over for a while before Neil said, "I hope you remember, Charlie. For your own sake."

CHAPTER TEN

The Principal

The teenagers left for school and arrived five minutes before the bell rang.

There was a school assembly today. Charlie was near the front of the auditorium. He normally sat at the back but this week the seating arrangements had changed. The principal walked in and stood at the podium at the front of the auditorium, his hands firmly clasping the edge of it. The principal spoke with a stern tone and pronounced each syllable with precision. The principal never seemed to laugh or smile.

Since being at the school, Charlie had never really seen the principal up close. The principal kept his distance from the students and was never really seen at school apart from assemblies. Charlie could never really make out the principal's face that well, since Charlie normally sat at the back. Now Charlie could see the principal up close. He had narrow and gaunt features. His hair was brown and his chin was shaved. His lips were very thin—almost to the point of non-existence.

As the principal droned on about the lack of discipline in schools nowadays, Charlie had a haunting feeling. The principal's face, his voice, they both nagged at Charlie, hinting at something that he could not quite grasp.

Then Charlie figured it out. The revelation came suddenly, as if a switch had been flipped in his brain. He hadn't believed it before because it had seemed so ridiculous.

The man was Edward P. Oates, the old principal!

Charlie frowned. The principal no longer had a beard, but he looked the same age as the person in the dream, so it couldn't be him.

Or maybe that was part of the evil magic? Charlie knew Edward P. Oates was a witch. Maybe he had sold his soul for eternal life?

Charlie took one last look at the principal before the assembly ended and he left the auditorium.

◉   ◉   ◉

After school, Charlie met up with Kate and Neil.

"I think I know who the person is that Oates reminds me of," Charlie said.

"Who?" asked Kate.

Charlie told Kate and Neil about the assembly and how sure he was that he was correct. When he finished, Kate said, "Charlie, that's the wildest thing I've ever heard."

"Are you sure, Kate?" asked Charlie. "You're forgetting that we are on a ghost hunt."

Kate sighed and said, "So what do we do now?"

"Let's go look at the hallway photos."

"Fine," answered Kate.

Back in school, they made their way into the hall with all of the school's principals. There were still students walking around the halls, so they didn't look out of place.

They reached Edward's photograph and Kate and Neil took a good look at it. After this photograph there were eight others.

"Oh my gosh!" gasped Charlie, looking at the other photographs. "Look at them!"

Kate and Neil quickly looked at the next eight photographs and studied them for a while, not finding anything particularly out of the ordinary with them. Until Kate, then Neil, figured it out.

"I don't believe it," cried Kate, her words streaming out of her mouth at a rapid pace.

"That's freaky," Neil said in a quivering voice.

"You can see it too?" asked Charlie.

"Of course we can," replied Neil. "The principals are all the same person!"

"The eyes, sharp cheekbones, and thin lips give

it away," said Charlie.

"I'm surprised nobody's noticed before," said Neil.

"So am I," said Charlie. "But I guess it's true we only noticed because we looked at them so closely."

"So this means that these principals are all just old Ed?" asked Neil.

"I wonder if any other photos before Edward's are the same man?" asked Kate.

"No," replied Neil, "Edward Oates is the first."

"I wonder who the other people are," said Charlie. "I get the feeling that they may just be teachers or something."

"I don't want to think about it." Kate shivered.

"It explains why the older teachers are so freaky—they're witches!" joked Neil.

"Ha ha, you're so funny," said Charlie sarcastically.

"I wish we went to a normal school," Kate sighed. "There's no way all schools are like this."

CHAPTER ELEVEN

All of Us

Back home, Charlie decided to do some more work on his story, which he had neglected recently. The extra writing which appeared when Charlie was asleep had stopped since the teenagers had begun to investigate, so Charlie was surprised to find a new entry.

He quickly showed it to his brother and sister.

*The boy and his helpers were in danger—
the witch knew everything and was now
out to silence them so they would not tell others
of the actions of the witch and his acolytes.*

"What's an acolyte?" asked Neil.

"A sort of assistant," Charlie told him. "This is a warning."

"What should we do?" asked Kate.

"Stay inside and be careful," said Charlie.

"I'm scared, Charlie," stated Kate.

"We'll pull through, Kate," Charlie told her.

"I hope so, Charlie," Kate said.

They decided to watch a movie before going to bed early. Soon they were all asleep, cozy in their beds.

For once Charlie did not have his dream, but his sleep was sporadic.

Suddenly he awoke with a start and sat up. He had heard his name being called. He looked around but saw nothing, so he slowly rested his head upon his pillow again and closed his eyes. Then he heard it again. He sat up and looked around for the source of the voice. The wind was blowing through the leaves outside and Charlie listened to it carefully. It sounded like someone whispering, "Charlie, Charlie," again and again.

Charlie frowned. If the wind was blowing he would have heard the oak tree tapping the window. Also he would be able to see it shaking in the moonlight. He sat up again and looked out of the window at the still tree. Slowly, horror began to crawl through his body and a cold chill ran up his spine. The words on his notebook came back to haunt him.

Kate awoke. She felt someone's hand over her face. She opened her eyes but there was nothing. She decided that she had imagined it and tried to go back to sleep. Suddenly she felt it again and opened her eyes but saw nothing. Then she saw a man-shaped shadow in the corner and opened her mouth to scream.

Neil opened his eyes slowly. He heard a creak

from a floorboard. He looked in the direction of the sound, thinking Charlie or Kate had come into his room. Nobody was there. He shut his eyes again and decided that it must have been the floorboards settling.

Suddenly, he heard a shuffling sound on the other side of the bed. He opened his eyes again and looked in the sound's direction but still nothing. Just before he closed his eyes again, he saw a shadow in front of the window and then heard a loud scream coming from Kate's bedroom.

Charlie was about to turn his bedside light on when he heard Kate scream. He leapt from bed and ran out of the room.

In the hallway, Neil and Charlie came rushing out of their rooms and looked at each other briefly. Then they ran toward Kate's door just as Kate ran out of it.

"What's wrong, Kate?" asked Charlie.

"There was someone in my room," replied Kate.

"Yours too?" asked Neil. "There was someone in mine as well."

"And mine," said Charlie.

"A person in each of our rooms!" Neil cried. "Where did they come from?"

"I think they have something to do with the warning," Charlie explained. "I think that it was witchcraft or evil magic."

"So they weren't really there?" asked Kate.

"I don't think we will find anyone in there. I bet Oates is toying with us."

"Then what should we do?" asked Kate.

"Stop him," Charlie announced.

"How?" asked Neil.

"We go to the school. Right now. All of us. It's dangerous here if the guy is using magic," Charlie said.

CHAPTER TWELVE

The Contract

"I'll go upstairs and grab our clothes," said Charlie.

"I'll come too," Neil said.

"No," Charlie replied, "stay here with Kate."

"If you're sure," Neil said doubtfully.

"Look, I'll be fine!" Charlie told him. "You two find anything that we'll need to help us, like flashlights, for example."

"Okay, Charlie," Kate said. "Be careful."

"I'm only going upstairs," Charlie said over his shoulder as he trod on the first step. It creaked ominously. "Nothing's going to happen."

Charlie continued cautiously upstairs until he

reached the landing. He pressed the light switch.
Click! Nothing. Click! Click!

Charlie shrugged and proceeded down the
hallway slowly. He was trying to convince himself
that the light bulb had probably just blown and
that there was nothing to worry about. He didn't
find himself very convincing.

He went into his bedroom and pressed the
light switch. Again, nothing. There was a bright
blue flash at the window and then there was an
enormously loud rumble that seemed to shake the
house to its very foundation. Charlie jumped in
fright and then forced himself to relax.

Thunder and lightning, that's all it is, he
thought as he grabbed his clothes and ran into
Kate's room. He grabbed her clothes from her
chair where she had left them as another bolt of
lightning flashed outside, followed by another
almighty roar of thunder. He then went into Neil's
room. As he picked up Neil's T-shirt, he looked

at the window. Thin curtains were drawn over the window, but Charlie could still see the blue of the lightning's flash through them. Two lightning bolts flashed, followed almost instantly by rumbles of thunder. Then a third flashed, illuminating a shady figure. The window went dark almost immediately again before being illuminated by lightning. There was nothing there.

Charlie turned and ran toward the door, still holding the clothes. The figure was in the doorway with its hands outstretched. Charlie charged into it and headbutted it at the same time. As the figure fell back, Charlie kicked away its legs and ran down the stairs. The figure howled as it rolled around on the floor. Lightning flashed once, twice, three times, and the figure was gone.

Downstairs, Kate and Neil were waiting in the kitchen.

"I wonder what's keeping Charlie," said Neil.

"I don't know," replied Kate.

Suddenly there was a thump upstairs, followed by rapid footsteps echoing off of the stairs. Charlie burst in and fell against the table panting.

"Here," he said, gasping for breath, "put them on and let's go."

"What was all that thumping?" asked Kate.

"I saw a man in the window and by the door. He tried to grab me," Charlie replied, recovering a little.

"We should leave as soon as possible," Neil said as he put on his jeans.

"Well, I'm ready," Kate said.

"And so am I," said Charlie as he pulled his sweater over his head. "Come on, Neil."

"I'm ready," Neil answered.

The teenagers crept toward the front door. As they passed the hall closet on the way to the door, Neil stopped and opened it. He rummaged around inside until he pulled out a blue plastic baseball bat.

"It's not as good as a real bat, but it'll do," he whispered to Charlie.

"Anything else in there?" asked Charlie in a hushed voice.

"Let me see," replied Neil. He once again rummaged around until he found a tennis racket.

"I think there's another one as well," Neil said as he handed it to Charlie. "Ah, here it is."

He handed the other one to Kate who took it and sized it up in her hands.

"Thanks, Neil," she answered. "Just what I need for fighting the powers of evil."

"Better than nothing," Neil said.

"Come on, you two," Charlie said, pushing them forward.

The teenagers reached the front door, put their shoes on, and slowly let themselves out. They walked down the path in the rain and opened the gate. It creaked loudly and the teenagers winced.

The teenagers quickly and quietly ran down

the street in the direction of the school, peering furtively left and right, constantly on the lookout for anything out of the ordinary.

They arrived at the school and climbed through a gap in the fence which was situated in the middle of the school field. The field was muddy from the rain and in places the mud had turned to liquid, causing them to slip and slide as they walked.

They reached the old school building and walked along the wall, testing the windows to see if any opened. After about three minutes, they found one. It shuddered open and the teenagers quickly climbed in, one after another, each wielding their weapons. Once in, they weaved silently through the rows of chairs before reaching the door. Charlie opened the door a bit and they went through.

"Follow me and keep close to the wall," Charlie whispered to his brother and sister.

"Okay," replied Kate and Neil together.

The building was completely silent, except for

the quiet footsteps of the teenagers, which could only be heard if you listened very carefully.

As they approached the room, they saw a pale, flickering light. When they reached the door, they found that the light was coming from within and was shining through the glass panel in the upper half of the door. The light darkened occasionally as a person within the room moved past it.

Faint murmuring could be heard from the room as well as a voice slightly louder than the rest. The voice was chanting something. There were several bright flashes and a strange clicking sound was heard, which slowly died away, leaving just the murmuring and chanting again.

Charlie motioned for Kate and Neil to stay where they were and slowly moved forward so that he could just peer in through the glass.

Inside was the scene from his dream. There were thick yellow candles, the star on the floor, and the robed figures on each corner. Then there was the sixth figure—the principal.

Inside the star, sparks suddenly appeared which slowly multiplied until there was a bright fiery column. Blue light flashed within the center of the column.

The principal raised his hands above his head and chanted something in a loud voice. An image slowly began to form within the column of light and Charlie began to make out three figures. Two were crouching next to each other and a third was leaning forward, peering through something.

It was them! Charlie suddenly realized that the image was of him and his brother and sister.

Charlie said to Neil, "Let's go in. They're onto us!"

"Stay there, Kate," Neil said.

"No way! I'm going in," she responded.

"No, don't—it's too dangerous."

"I don't care," she replied.

"Now," cried Charlie.

He tore open the door and ran in, followed by Kate, and then Neil.

Charlie ran into one of the figures and pushed them into the middle of the group. The figure became a shadow before disappearing with a flash of light.

Neil, meanwhile, had hit one of the figures over the head with his bat. The figure staggered forward before collapsing onto the floor, unconscious. Kate had also hit someone with her tennis racket and the figure stumbled a little and fell, their hood falling from their head. The figure was a woman. Kate instantly recognized her. It was the head of the math department, Mrs. Briggs.

"My ankle—it's twisted," she cried.

"Mrs. Briggs! What are you doing?" exclaimed Kate. "Why are you doing this?"

Mrs. Briggs looked up at Kate with anger.

"Kate, what are you doing here? What you are doing is against school rules!"

"And what you're doing isn't?" asked Kate in disgust, before turning away and hitting someone who was about to grab her. The person collapsed onto the floor, writhing in agony.

Charlie had just hit someone with a chair, having lost his racket in the column of light. The person whom he had just hit staggered backwards into the wall and slid down.

During all this, the principal was calm. He raised his right hand into the air and muttered something. Sulfur colored fire burst forth from his fingertips and spiraled toward Neil. He raised his plastic bat and shielded himself. The bat melted and Neil instantly let go of the burning plastic.

"Ouch!" cried Neil, leaping behind the desk.

Kate ran toward the principal with her racket raised. The principal raised an eyebrow. Kate was lifted from her feet and pinned halfway up the opposite wall. The principal laughed and looked around for Charlie, who had just made it out of the door. A trail of yellow fire followed him and burst against the wall in the hallway, leaving a red circle that glowed and burned the paint.

"I'll get you later, foolish boy," hissed the principal in a fearsome voice.

Neil furtively opened drawers behind the desk in search of a weapon. He tore a drawer right out and hurled it over the desk in the shallow hope that it may just hit the raving principal. It did with a heavy thud that sent the principal staggering, but unfortunately didn't stop or injure him. The principal raised his hand to emit another fireball, this time at the desk. The blue fireball ripped through the air with a terrible sizzling, roaring noise. It hit the desk and bathed it in a soft, blue bubble of light. Neil kicked himself away just in time. All the corners and edges of the desk became outlined in thin lines of dazzling orange before the entire desk exploded with an almighty force. The force blasted Neil against the wall, knocking him unconscious. The principal left Neil and quickly exited the room in search of Charlie.

Charlie meanwhile was on his way to the science department. He burst into the first room he came across and went over to the cabinets in the corner. He opened them one by one, but they only contained graduated cylinders and other such items.

"Shoot," said Charlie quietly. "They're in the lab room!" Charlie left and made his way to the lab room at the end of the hall.

The room was quiet for a moment. The only sound was coming from the one opened cabinet swinging slightly from where Charlie had searched it in his haste. On the opposite wall, a shape began pushing through the plaster. The shape was a giant face that began to take the shape of the principal's face, but it was completely white. Suddenly the eyes became real and they looked around the room. The head stretched the wall as it peered left and right before sinking back into the plaster, until nothing was left except a plain white wall.

The principal stalked along the hallway, the darkness presenting no barrier as he pursued Charlie. He closed his eyes for a moment, muttered, and then opened them again. The eyes seemed to be looking at things other than what was ahead of him.

"So that's what he's up to…" the principal muttered in his inhuman voice. "How innnnteresting."

Charlie burst into the lab room in a panic. He had wasted too much time already. Charlie fumbled around drawers, looking for chemicals. He found a drawer with a pot of blue powder. Copper something. He didn't have time to look. He rapidly opened other drawers until he came across what he wanted. Potassium.

From what Charlie remembered from his science class, potassium was very reactive with water and air, which was the reason it was generally stored in kerosene. If Charlie used what was in this drawer, he might just defeat the principal.

Charlie took ten jars filled with kerosene and potassium out of the drawer. Charlie hastily unscrewed the jars and picked up some tweezers. He picked up each lump of potassium and transferred them all into a single jar. He must have had about a pound in all. He hoped it would be enough. He filled up a tray of water and set it on the floor in the hallway just before the doorway. Charlie then filled up a bucket with water and covered the floor just in case things went wrong. He knew he needed as much water as possible to react with the potassium.

Charlie knew that this was a long shot, but he had to try anyway. He wondered how his brother and sister were doing and hoped that the principal had left them alone.

Suddenly, Charlie heard a shuffling sound

coming from somewhere in the hallway.

There was a splash and a yell, and the shuffling stopped. Charlie leapt from inside the lab room and poured the potassium onto the tray of water in which the principal was standing, his eyes glowing that fearsome yellow.

"See ya, Principal Oates!" quipped Charlie as he ran down the hallway. The potassium burned fiercely in the water. The principal's robe set alight and soon he was engulfed in a fireball.

Charlie could hear an ear-piercing scream from behind him. He turned and gasped. The principal was growing bigger and bigger. His robe ripped, revealing a bright red torso. The principal grew talons and his head became distorted and ugly. His whole body was flame red!

"I wiillll gettttt youuu, Charrrlieee!" screamed the principal in a rage, stepping through the charred ruins of the hallway.

Flames licked the ceiling and soon the heat

grew unbearable. Charlie ran and ran while fireballs whizzed by him from the enraged demon the principal had become. The principal laughed maniacally. His now wide and armored shoulders scraped along the hallway walls, leaving long scratch marks in their wake.

Charlie reached a door and had just gotten through when a dark green streak of fire burst violently against it, melting the glass panel and atomizing the wood.

Charlie screamed and ran through another door, this one leading outside.

He ran like the wind across the school courtyard, feeling very exposed. If only he could find something—anything—to fight him off with.

Suddenly, Charlie tripped and stumbled and then tripped again. As he fell, he twisted and saw the demon towering above him, wrath glowing in its eyes. Long, black blades extended through the demon's charred hands.

"Yooouuu wiiillll suuuuffffeeerrr, Charrrlieeee!" the demon screeched.

Charlie closed his eyes for what he thought was the last time, thinking of what to say before he died.

"AAARRRGGGHH!" the demon screamed suddenly.

Charlie opened his eyes and looked up as the demon looked down at him and then turned around to see Neil through the slowly disappearing demon. The former principal tried to strike Neil but his hand went harmlessly through him. The demon tried a spell but all that came out was a puff of smoke from beneath his fingernails. He looked at them in disbelief and then looked at Neil.

"Hoowww diiddd yoouuu knooww?" he asked.

"I found the contract in your desk," replied Neil.

The demon screamed as he slowly shrank back into the form of the principal. The principal was nearly transparent, but he managed to get one more message for Neil and Charlie.

"Watch your back! I will return!" he said before completely disappearing.

Charlie looked at Neil. Neil looked at Charlie.

"Come on," said Neil, pulling Charlie up. "Let's find Kate and go home."

They found Kate in the classroom where they had left her. The remaining hooded figures, whom Charlie assumed were teachers, were all gone, as were the pillar of light and the chalk star. The teenagers looked at each other.

"Are you okay?" Charlie asked Kate.

"I'm okay, Charlie. I'm just a bit bruised, that's all," replied Kate.

"I'm so glad you're okay."

"Charlie?" Kate said.

"Yes?"

"Is he gone?"

"Ask Neil."

"Neil?"

They both looked at Neil.

"Go on, Neil," Kate said. "Please."

"Okay, okay," said Neil.

And so Neil told them about how the principal had left him unconscious and how he had recovered moments later. He had looked for the principal's office and had gone inside to look for something that would stop him. He looked inside a cabinet and found an ancient wooden box. He opened it and found a document. The contract. Signed in blood. The principal's blood!

"What did it say?" asked Kate, sitting on the edge of her chair in eagerness.

"It said," began Neil, pulling a sheet of paper from his pocket. "Well, you can read it yourself."

Charlie and Kate read the words together.

I, Edward Peter Oates, hereby swear that on this day I will part with my ethereal spirit, to give to the Prince of Darkness, Lord of the Underworld. In return for this, he will pledge that I will be granted everlasting life, unless one of the following situations occur. If any of these situations occur, the Prince of Darkness will be granted the right to take my soul without ever granting me everlasting life. Also, if one of the following situations occurred my existence in the Land of the Living will be terminated, and I will no longer have existed and no mortal will ever have remembered me.

These are the situations by which the contract will be broken: If I attempt to nullify the contract after the act of signing by any means. If I attempt to prevent the transaction taking place at the set time. If I ever come in contact with the spell contained in the glass vial, carried in the same box as this contract. Should I ever come into contact with this, the previous conditions will occur, as required by the Prince of Darkness, Lord of the Underworld, so that this contract is as fair to him, as it is to me.

Signed: Edward P. Oates.

Signed: P. of D., L. of the U.

"Wow!" exclaimed Charlie. "Great work, Neil."

"Very impressive, Neil," said Kate.

"Well," said Neil modestly, "I couldn't have done it without Charlie fending the guy off. It was nothing, really."

The teenagers went home joyously and made their way inside and upstairs silently. They were exhausted after their adventure and all they wanted to do was curl up and go to bed.

CHAPTER THIRTEEN

Another Dream

That night, Charlie didn't dream his normal dream, but another dream.

He was sitting in the dining room at the window seat when someone came in through the door. Charlie looked around and saw a man in a flat cap and tweed jacket walk toward him. The man had greasy hair sticking out at crazy angles from beneath the hat. Charlie knew who he was.

"Hello," Charlie said.

"Hello," replied the man, "I would just like to thank you for what you and your brother and sister did. Without you, I would have had to haunt this place forever, but now I am free. I don't quite know what will happen next but it can't be worse than the loneliness I have suffered since I died."

"The contract said the principal will have never existed," said Charlie. "What did it mean by that?"

"I don't know," answered the man truthfully. "But perhaps it means that I was never murdered and I will now live my life to the fullest."

"I hope so," Charlie said.

"But if that happens," said the man, "you may never live here."

"Sell it then," Charlie said.

"You're right, of course!" said the man. "You may get a new room in your kitchen. Tomorrow, go take a look behind those shelves again."

"All right," replied Charlie.

The man smiled before suddenly saying, "My word, what's happening?"

He was slowly disappearing like the principal did, and then he was gone, but not before he could say in an increasingly fading voice, "Thank you so much. I won't forget you three."

"What's your name?" asked Charlie suddenly.
"We never found out what your name was!"

"Robert. Robert Eves."

And then he was gone.

←   🕐   ←

1905

Robert awoke with a start. What a horrible
dream, but it had a happy ending. He would have
to write it down. It would make a great story.
He sat up from his place at the window seat and
looked outside. Up the path walked the mail
carrier, carrying just one letter.

Robert went to the door, greeted the mail
carrier, and took the letter. Then he went inside
and sat down and opened the envelope with a
knife. Inside was a letter with the school emblem.

*Congratulations on your promotion to
the position of principal, Mr. Eves, a job which*

I am sure you will be well equipped to do.
You have a salary increase of...

Robert sat back in his chair in triumph. So he had gotten the job instead of Mr. Oates.

Hang on, he thought. Who was Mr. Oates?

→ 🕐 →

Present

Charlie woke up feeling great. In fact, he had never felt better. He woke up his siblings and they all went downstairs and sat at the kitchen table.

"I can't believe last night really happened," said Charlie.

"Me either," said Neil.

"I had another dream, though," Charlie added.

Neil groaned. "So it's not over?" he asked.

"Oh, it's over, but the teacher, Robert Eves, thanked us for what we did."

Kate smiled and asked, "So what happened?"

"I'll tell you all about it," said Charlie.

Be sure to check out the othe

Pen Pals
ISBN: 9781486718757

The Scarecrow
ISBN: 9781486718788

Stage Fright
ISBN: 9781486718771

Ghost Writer
ISBN: 9781486721269